Lucy lives at
64 Zoo Lane,
right next door
to the zoo. Every
night, she climbs
out of her window,
slides down the long
long neck of Georgina
the Giraffe and listens to
one of the animals
tell her a story . . .

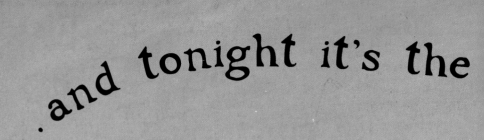

...and tonight it's the

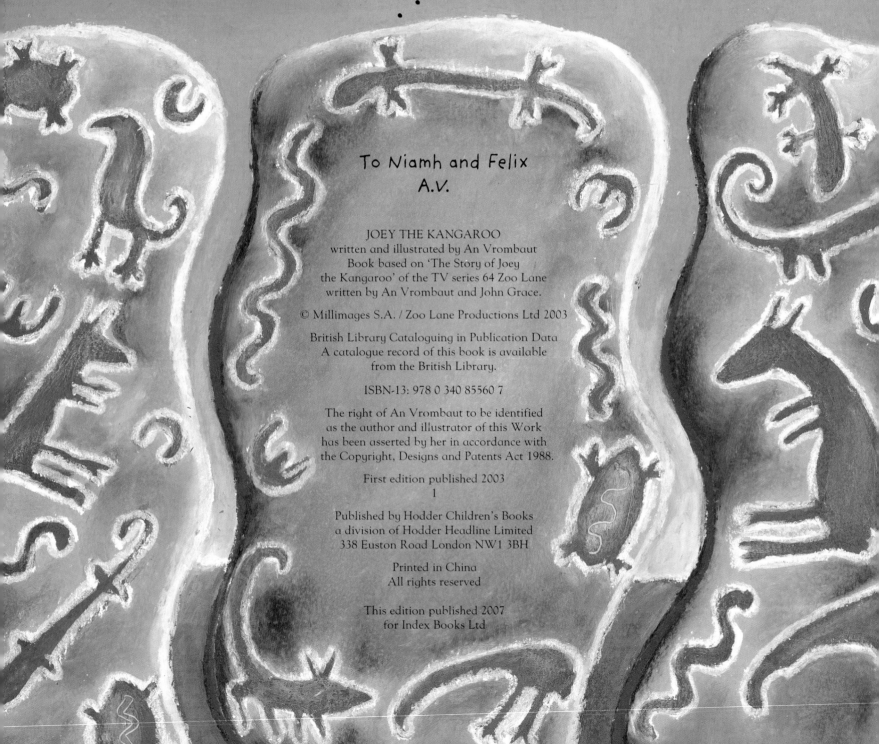

To Niamh and Felix
A.V.

JOEY THE KANGAROO
written and illustrated by An Vrombaut
Book based on 'The Story of Joey
the Kangaroo' of the TV series 64 Zoo Lane
written by An Vrombaut and John Grace.

© Millimages S.A. / Zoo Lane Productions Ltd 2003

British Library Cataloguing in Publication Data
A catalogue record of this book is available
from the British Library.

ISBN-13: 978 0 340 85560 7

The right of An Vrombaut to be identified
as the author and illustrator of this Work
has been asserted by her in accordance with
the Copyright, Designs and Patents Act 1988.

First edition published 2003
1

Published by Hodder Children's Books
a division of Hodder Headline Limited
338 Euston Road London NW1 3BH

This edition published 2007
for Index Books Ltd

story of

Joey the Kangaroo

An Vrombaut

Hodder
Children's
Books

A division of Hachette Children's Books

In Australia, in the shadow of the Great Red Rock, lived a little kangaroo called Joey. He was too small to jump by himself, but Joey didn't mind. Mum's pouch was safe and comfy . . . just right for a baby kangaroo!

Weeks and months passed by.
Then came spring, and all over Australia
little kangaroos were learning to jump.

'We're practising for the Junior Jump!' said Jimmy
while he bounced up and down.
'I bet you can't jump as high as me!'

Joey tried . . .

But ... **PLOOF!** He fell down in the dust.
'Joey's got flat feet!' Jimmy laughed.

All the little roos joined in singing:

'JOEY CA-AN'T JU-UMP!
JOEY CA-AN'T JU-UMP!'

Joey walked home, dragging his feet in the sand.

His dad was waiting for him. 'Look, son!' he said and made a mighty leap. 'Now, show me you can jump like your dad!'

Joey tried and tried, but he couldn't lift his feet off the ground.

Then . . .

PLOOF!

Joey fell down again.

'Blundering boomerangs!' groaned Joey's dad. 'I've never seen a kangaroo who can't jump!'

When night fell, Joey slipped away
to the billabong. He sat on a rock,
feeling sad and lonely.

Plip, plop, plip, plop . . .

Joey's teardrops fell into the water.

'Oh my, oh my, I'm getting a bit wet down here!' gurgled a voice from the billabong. 'The rainy season has come early!'

And then . . .
RIBIT!
. . .out jumped a frog.

'What's the matter, little roo?'
asked the frog, when he saw Joey.
'I can't jump,' sobbed Joey.
'No worries!' croaked Ribit.

He plunged back into the billabong
and fished out a pair of yellow boots.

'These boots helped me
to jump when I was
a little tadpole.
You can borrow
them if you like.'

Joey tried on Ribit's
jumping boots.
He closed his eyes.
At first nothing happened,
but then he felt a tickle in his feet.
A tickle that made him jump up!
'I DID IT!' cheered Joey.
All night he practised with Ribit,
jumping higher and
higher and higher!

And when the sun rose
over the Great Red Rock,
it was the day of the Junior Jump.
All the little roos had come to the
billabong with their mums and dads,
grannies, granddads, aunties and uncles.

The little roos took turns to jump over a stick.
Jimmy did a triple backward
upside-down jump.

Then it was Joey's turn.

He jumped up . . . and up . . . and up . . . and up . . .

...higher than ALL the other little roos!

'HOORAY!'

cheered Joey's mum and dad.

But Jimmy pointed at Joey's boots.
'Hey, that's not fair!' he said.
'Joey's wearing special boots.'

'You're right,' said Mr Platypus.
'Sorry Joey, jumping boots are not allowed.
You'll have to jump without them.'

Joey was scared. He wasn't sure he could do it.

'No worries,' whispered Ribit. 'Those boots are beginner's boots. You don't need them anymore!'

So Joey kicked off the boots. He took a deep breath and started to bounce.

Up and down ... up and down ... up and down ...

Joey could feel the tickle in his feet getting stronger and stronger and stronger ...

Until he jumped over the stick and up into the sky!

'The winner of the Junior Jump is . . . **Joey!**' announced Mr Platypus.

Joey's mum and dad were
so proud they leapt for joy.
Everyone joined in, skipping
and hopping and bouncing . . .

Even Jimmy – because he could feel
a tickle in his feet too!